ARTEMIS FOWL

THE GRAPHIC NOVEL

Adapted by

EOIN COLFER
&
ANDREW DONKIN

Art by GIOVANNI RIGANO
Color by PAOLO LAMANNA

HYPERION BOOKS FOR CHILDREN
New York

How does one describe Artemis Fowl?
Various psychiatrists have tried and
failed. The main problem is Artemis's own
intelligence. He bamboozles every test
thrown at him. He has puzzled the greatest
medical minds and sent many of them
gibbering to their own hospitals.

There is no doubt that Artemis is a
child prodigy. But why does someone of such
brilliance dedicate himself to criminal
activities? This is a question that can
be answered by only one person. And he
delights in not talking.

Perhaps the best way to create an accurate
picture of Artemis is to tell the by now
famous account of his first villainous
venture. I have put together this report
from firsthand interviews with the victims,
and as the tale unfolds you will realize
that this was not easy.

This story began several years ago at
the dawn of the twenty-first century.
Artemis Fowl had devised a plan to
restore his family's fortune. A plan that
could topple civilizations and plunge the
planet into a cross-species war.

He was twelve years old at the time. . . .

CHAPTER 1:
THE BOOK

Of course, it had started with the Internet. But then it always does.

Alien abductions. UFO sightings. Ley lines. Ancient stone circles.

And the People. It always came back to the People.

Trawling through gigs of data, he had compiled a database from the thousands of references to fairies he'd found from countries all over the world.

Each human civilization had its own term for the People. But there was no doubt that the reports referred to the same hidden race.

Many stories whispered of a special book carried by each fairy.

It was their Bible, containing the history of their race. It also contained their laws, their rules... and their weaknesses.

Any human who came into possession of such a book would have an entirely new species to exploit.

Of course, this book was said to be written in Gnommish, so even if someone could steal a copy, it would be of absolutely no use to any human.

NAME:
Artemis Fowl the Second

CLASSIFICATION:
VERY DANGEROUS

KNOWN PSEUDONYMS AND ALIASES:
Dr. F. Roy Dean Schlippe, Stefan Bashkir,
Emmsey Squire

SPECIALIZED SKILLS:
Possibly possesses the greatest human intellect
of his generation

*Perhaps any generation,
but you can't believe
everything he says.*

NAME:
Butler

FIRST NAME:
D CENSORED

CLASSIFICATION:
Bodyguard

BACKGROUND:
The Butlers have been serving the Fowls for centuries.
Several eminent linguists believe this is how the noun originated.

SPECIALIZED SKILLS:
SAS-level marksmanship, martial arts including Cos Ta'pa, emergency
medicine, information technology, and Cordon Bleu cooking. The subject
is fluent in several languages. Believed to have studied extensively
under the Japanese sensei Madame Ko. Spent several years working
freelance in the espionage arena, including stints for the British
and French secret service.

DISTINGUISHING FEATURES:
Blue diamond tattoo on shoulder

WEAPON OF CHOICE:
Sig Sauer

KNOWN ALIASES:
Constantin Bashkir, Colonel Xavier Lee

KNOWN RELATIONS:
Juliet—younger sister
"The Major"—his uncle, believed to have been killed when the CENSORED

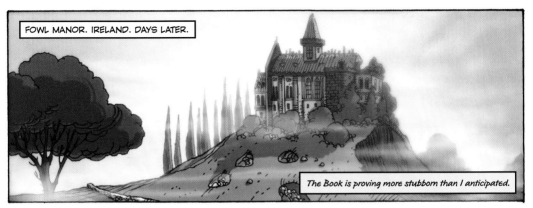

FOWL MANOR. IRELAND. DAYS LATER.

The Book is proving more stubborn than I anticipated.

CHAPTER 2:
TRANSLATION

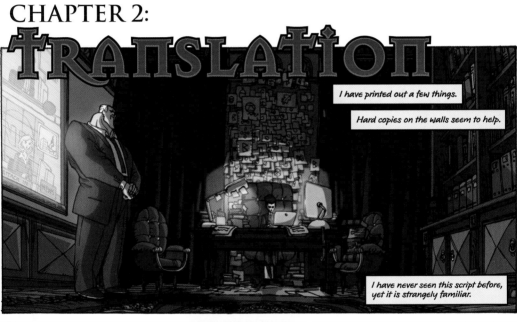

I have printed out a few things.

Hard copies on the walls seem to help.

I have never seen this script before, yet it is strangely familiar.

...And so Chicago's district attorney had to watch yet again as Mr. Spiro walked free from court. Problems here proving difficult to solve.

The text meanders around the page in no apparent order.

Juliet. Butler's little sister.

ARTEMIS? IT'S...IT'S MRS. FOWL. SHE'S ASKING FOR... SOMEONE.

Mother. I leave the computer comparing every symbol in the Book with every letter in every modern language in the entire world.

I don't think it's going to work.

MOTHER? ARE YOU AWAKE?

OF COURSE, I'M AWAKE. HOW CAN I SLEEP IN THIS BLINDING GLARE?

NEGATIVE

ARTEMIS, DARLING, WHERE HAVE YOU BEEN?

SCHOOL TRIP, MOTHER. SKIING IN AUSTRIA.

NEGATIVE

WOULD YOU CLOSE THOSE WRETCHED CURTAINS? THE LIGHT IS INTOLERABLE.

Egyptian.

The first written human stories were about fairies, suggesting that their civilization predated man's. It would seem that the Egyptians had simply adapted an existing script to create their own.

I feel a tightness of anticipation in my chest. Unusual.

IT'S JUST AFTER DAWN, SIR. WHY DON'T YOU HAVE A BREAK?

I'M NEARLY FINISHED, BUTLER. TURN OFF THE TELEVISIONS, WOULD YOU? I NEED QUIET TO FINISH THE TRANSLATION.

SIR, THE TELEVISIONS HAVEN'T BEEN OFF FOR OVER A YEAR. IF THERE IS NEWS OF MR. FOWL SENIOR BEING RECOVERED, THEN IT'S BOUND TO BE ON THERE FIRST.

But there isn't going to be any news of Mr. Fowl.

BARENTS SEA

PENINSULA OF KOLA

FINLAND

Censored

ARTEMIS FOWL SENIOR

NAME:
Artemis Fowl Senior

FAMILY MOTTO:
Aurum potestas est (Gold is power.)

BACKGROUND:
Head of a criminal empire that stretched from Dublin's docklands to the backstreets of Tokyo. Fowl Senior also had ambitions to establish himself as a legitimate businessman.

KNOWN RELATIONS:
Angeline Fowl—wife and mother of Artemis Fowl II

RECENT HISTORY:
Bought a cargo ship and stocked it with 250,000 cans of cola and set course for Murmansk in northern Russia. The ship, the Fowl Star, was sunk in the Bay of Kola by a stolen Stinger missile fired by the Russia Mafiya. Artemis Fowl Senior was reported missing, presumed dead. CENSORED ORED in a ravine south of the harbor.

IF I WAS ONE OF YOUR PRECIOUS SPRITES, WE WOULDN'T EVEN BE HAVING THIS CONVERSATION.

DON'T YOU DARE IMPLY...

Too far.

INCOMING EMERGENCY TRANSMISSION. PRIORITY ONE!

Commander Root, we have an emergency. We have a runner. Southern Italy. No shield. Human contact in minutes.

The bad news— it's a rogue troll.

Trolls are the meanest of the deep-tunnel creatures. They wander the labyrinth, preying on anything unlucky enough to cross their path.

Their tiny brains have no room for rules or restraint. Very occasionally, one gets to the surface. When they do, it's a disaster.

YOU RUNNING HOT?

I'm so far behind with the Ritual that I can't remember how long it's been. But if I say that, I'm finished. I nod and I lie.

BE CAREFUL WHAT YOU WISH FOR, OFFICER SHORT. LOOKS LIKE YOU GOT YOUR CHANCE. LOCATE THE TROLL. THEN WAIT—I SAID WAIT—FOR THE RETRIEVAL TEAM. GOT THAT?

"You ever seen what an angry troll can do to flesh and bone?"

"No, sir."

"Good. Keep it that way. Now, move."

Most of all, don't think about the gray stain.

Don't think about the swirling, hissing magma searching your craft for a weak spot.

Don't think about the MACH 2 force trying to turn you inside out.

Don't think about the half-melted rocks beating against the sides.

Don't think about the white-hot magma flow engulfing you.

NAME:
Captain Holly Short

CLASSIFICATION:
Elf. Also first and only female Recon officer assigned to the LEPrecon—
an elite branch of the Lower Elements Police

BACKGROUND:
Subject is a city elf born and bred in Haven City. Like all elves,
she has the fairy powers of healing, the <u>mesmer</u>, shielding (from
human sight), as well as the gift of tongues.

CAREER:
Top pilot in her class at the Academy, where she studied under Wing
Commander Vinyáya. Worked traffic detail (nicknamed Wheelies) for
six months. Earned her silver acorns during highly controversial
initiation on the island of Tern Mor, off the Irish coast CENSORED
CENSORED ENSORED RED Turnball Root. CENSORED

Her early career in Recon was blighted by the notorious "Hamburg
Incident." A CENSORED fled to the surface and attempted to bargain
with a group of sinister human occultists who were using CENSORED
The cross-species fallout from Holly's intervention resulted in four
full memory wipes, one time-stop, and several cases of permanent
insanity among the humans involved. [Also see the classified Section
Eight CENSORED "The Hamburg Incident: Applied Evil."]

WEAPON OF CHOICE:
Neutrino3000

CHAPTER 4:

ONE HOUR AGO.

I head for the old country.

Butler prepares the field kit.

Mirrored sunglasses. Two pairs.

Portable radar.

NAME:
Fowl Manor

LOCATION:
A two-hundred-acre estate on the outskirts of Dublin, Ireland

BACKGROUND:
Records show the original Fowl castle was built by Lord Hugh Fowl
in the fifteenth century. It overlooks low-lying land on all sides.
Over the centuries, the castle was remodeled until it became the
manor that stands today. Fowl Manor has survived war, civil unrest,
and several tax audits.

Used on sunday

Found on the gravel drive

DOCTOR PO
ST. BARTLEBY'S SCHOOL FOR YOUNG GENTLEMEN
COUNTY WICKLOW, IRELAND.

CHAPTER 5:

MISSING IN ACTION

DUBLIN DOCKS.

"A diversion then, Butler. Two minutes are all I need."

EVENING, LADIES. ISN'T IT A BIT LATE FOR BLOUSE-WEARING GIRLS LIKE YOU TO BE OUT? DO YOUR MOTHERS KNOW? OR ARE THEY TOO DRUNK BY THIS TIME OF NIGHT?

AND HERE'S THE WORST BIT.

IT GETS WORSE?

JUST BEFORE HOLLY DROPS THE HELMET, THERE'S A GLINT OF LIGHT IN THE FRAME. I SLOWED DOWN THE IMAGE. LOOK...

"Oh no."

POLICE!

EEEEEEEEEEE!
EEEEEEEEEEE!

TELL ME WE STILL HAVE HER LOCATOR SIGNAL?

LOUD AND CLEAR. GOT A STRONG SIGNAL MOVING NORTH AT ABOUT EIGHTY KLICKS AN HOUR.

GO TO FULL ALERT. GET RETRIEVAL OUT OF THEIR BUNKS AND PREP THEM FOR A SURFACE SHOT.

I WANT FULL TACTICAL AND A COUPLE OF TECHIES. YOU TOO, FOALY. WE MAY HAVE TO STOP TIME ON THIS ONE.

FOR A JOB LIKE THIS, WE NEED OUR VERY BEST.

YOU WANT ME TO CALL IN CAPTAIN VEIN?

NO, FOALY, I'M TALKING ABOUT ME. GET ME A POD READY.

"I'm leaving on the next magma flare."

Nicknamed "Beetroot" by his staff.

NAME:
Julius Root

CLASSIFICATION:
LEPrecon commander—known for his liking of noxious fungus cigars

BACKGROUND:
A career cop. He has little respect for authority apart from his own.
Has commandeered the Atlantean ambassador's shuttle on more than one
occasion leading to minor diplomatic incidents. Head of Recon for many
decades—a high pressure job given that Recon is a notoriously dangerous
posting with a high fatality rate.

WEAPON OF CHOICE:
Multiphase, water-cooled, tri-barreled blaster

KNOWN RELATIONS:
Older brother—Captain Turnball Root CENSORED ENSORED exile

3a.m. Time, I think, for a little chat with our guest.

ARTEMIS? *ARTEMIS!*

CHAPTER 6:

SIEGE

ARTEMIS... IT'S YOUR MOTHER.

I feel a lead ball drop in my stomach.

MADAM FOWL SAYS THAT YOUR FATHER IS BACK. SHE SAYS HE'S COME HOME!

Guilt tears at my insides. I've been thinking about our little fairy friends so much that I had given up.

DID YOU SEE HIM, JULIET? WITH YOUR OWN EYES?

NO, ARTEMIS, SIR. I DID HEAR VOICES, THOUGH, FROM HER BEDROOM.

I take the stairs two at a time.

Is it possible?

MOTHER? I'M COMING IN.

FREEZE, MUD BOY. JUST GIVE ME A REASON.

THIS ENOUGH REASON?

SLAPPP!

SCARED, CERTAINLY. DEAD? PROBABLY NOT. MISSION ACCOMPLISHED.

AND THAT'S HANDY. ONE OF YOU IS STILL AWAKE.

GULP!

NAME?

GRUB... ER... I MEAN CORPORAL KELP.

WELL, CORPORAL, I HAVE A VERY IMPORTANT MESSAGE FOR YOU TO TAKE BACK TO YOUR COMMANDING OFFICER. ARE YOU LISTENING CAREFULLY?

YOU TELL YOUR COMMANDER THAT THE NEXT TIME I SEE ARMED FORCES COMING IN HERE, THEY'LL BE PICKED OFF BY SNIPER FIRE.

EVEN MORE IMPORTANT, I WANT A NEGOTIATOR SENT IN. SOMEONE WHO CAN ACTUALLY MAKE DECISIONS. GOT IT?

HERE IS THE SITUATION AS I SEE IT.

I HAVE THE MEANS TO EXPOSE YOUR SUBTERRANEAN EXISTENCE, AND YOU ARE POWERLESS TO STOP ME.

SO, BASICALLY, WHATEVER I ASK FOR IS A SMALL PRICE TO PAY.

YOU THINK YOU CAN JUST PUT ALL THIS INFORMATION OUT OVER THE INTERNET?

NOT WITH YOUR TIME-STOP IN EFFECT, NO.

WELL, IF YOU KNOW ABOUT THE TIME-STOP, THEN YOU MUST ALSO KNOW THAT YOU ARE COMPLETELY CUT OFF FROM THE OUTSIDE WORLD. YOU ARE POWERLESS.

LET'S SAVE SOME TIME HERE.

I GROW WEARY OF YOUR CLUMSY BLUFFS.

I KNOW THAT IN THE CASE OF AN ABDUCTION, THE LEP WILL FIRST SEND IN A CRACK RETRIEVAL TEAM.

EXCUSE ME WHILE I TITTER. CRACK TEAM? HONESTLY A CUB SCOUT PATROL ARMED WITH WATER PISTOLS COULD HAVE DEFEATED THEM.

THE NEXT STEP IN A TIME-STOP IS NEGOTIATION. IF THAT FAILS, THEN A BIO-BOMB IS DETONATED.

SO, LET'S HAVE IT. WHAT ARE YOUR DEMANDS?

ONE DEMAND. SINGULAR.

NAME:
Time-stops

BACKGROUND:
Fairies have been stopping time for millennia. Time-stops were traditionally initiated by five elfin warlocks who would form a pentagram around the target and spread an enchanted enclosure over it, temporarily stopping time inside. This was fine as far as it went, provided the warlocks didn't have to use the bathroom. Many a siege was lost because an elf had one glass of wine too many.

RECENT DEVELOPMENTS:
LEP technical genius, Foaly, is responsible for what we recognize as the modern time-stop. With humans developing satellite communication, today's time-stops need to be fine-tuned and precise. Foaly introduced the idea of warlocks storing their magic in lithium batteries—a move greatly resisted by powerful warlock unions at the time. Foaly then engineered a network of mobile receiver dishes that could be positioned around the designated area. These developments mean that sieges can now be extended for up to eight hours.

Bio-bombs—often used by the LEP in conjunction with time-stops. The bio-bomb kills all living things in a set radius, but leaves all other material intact. The radioactive element used in the core is solinium 2, which has a half-life of fourteen seconds.

HAVEN CITY.

A POLICE HOLDING CELL.

CHAPTER 7:

MULCH

YOU KNOW WHAT, MULCH DIGGUMS? THE POLICE MUST REALLY DISLIKE YOU.

WHY DO YOU SAY THAT?

FOUR GOBLINS. ONE DWARF. IF THEY LIKED YOU, THEY WOULDN'T PUT YOU IN HERE, WOULD THEY? WITH US.

GUESS THAT'S WHAT YOU GET WHEN YOU TRY TO STEAL YOUR ARRESTING OFFICER'S WATCH IN THE BOOKING LINE.

NOT THAT YOU SHOULD BE IN HERE WITH US. I THINK YOU STINKIN' DWARFS ARE DISGUSTING.

YOU TUNNEL BY UNHINGING YOUR JAWS, MUNCHING THROUGH SOIL AT A SUPER FAST RATE, AND THEN EJECTING IT FROM YOUR LOWER END. *UGH!*

I DON'T WANT ANY TROUBLE.

I BET YOU DON'T. WHICH IS A SHAME. FOR YOU, I MEAN.

YOU DWARFS DON'T LIKE FIRE MUCH, DO YOU?

"And don't you even think about trying to escape, convict! Remember, Foaly and I are watching you. The iris-cam shows us everything."

JULIUS? CAN YOU HEAR ME? I'M IN.

We hear you loud and clear.

DOOR'S LOCKED, BUT THE HUMANS HAVEN'T MADE A LOCK THAT CAN'T BE PICKED BY DWARF HAIR.

THREE CAMERAS ON THE CORRIDOR. NINETY-SECOND SWEEP. NO WAY THROUGH.

"Foaly here. Adjusting the iris-cam."

HANDY...

"OK, Mulch. It's a simple video network. I'm going to broadcast a loop of the last ten seconds to every camera from our dishes. Count to three, then move it."

WHATEVER YOU DID MUST HAVE WORKED.

I TELL YOU, JULIUS, AFTER ALL THAT TUNNELING, I GOT A VERY BAD CASE OF DWARF GAS BUILDING UP DOWN BELOW.

You are a disgusting individual, Diggums!

HEY, THERE'S A VASE IN HERE THAT LOOKS...

You're not in there to rob the place, Diggums. You're there to find out how Fowl knows so much about us.

THERE'S AN INTERESTING ROOM HERE, FOALY. MUST BE IMPORTANT. IT'S GOT THREE HIDDEN CAMERAS. I NEED TO KNOW EXACTLY WHERE THEY'RE POINTING. CAN YOU HELP?

This may sting a bit...

NOT BEHIND THE PICTURE. OH PLEASE.

BOOOM!

I'M COMING IN NOW, FAIRY GIRL, SO IF YOU'RE DOING ANYTHING EMBARRASSING, PLEASE STOP IT.

WHERE ARE...

WHY DON'T YOU TAKE OFF THOSE GLASSES, JULIET? THEY REALLY DON'T SUIT YOU.

I'LL TAKE OFF THESE GLASSES. THEY REALLY DON'T SUIT ME.

THAT'S BETTER. NOW I'VE GOT A FEW QUESTIONS FOR YOU.

Things are not good.

The manor's security has been compromised by an unsightly creature in leather pants.

The safe room has been blown apart by some sort of unwelcome fairy flatulence.

The same gaseous anomaly has also rendered Butler unconscious for a time.

And the People have retrieved the copy of the Book from the hidden safe.

I will have to dig very deep to uncover the good in this particular scenario.

I take several deep breaths. I focus. I find my chi.

Just as Butler always taught me.

I realize... I realize that what has happened means very little to the overall strategies of either side.

The People have recovered only one of several copies I have made of the Book.

Captain Short is still trapped in the manor.

The time-stop is still running out.

Soon the LEP would have no other option than to launch their bio-bomb and then, then I will deliver my coup de grace.

Of course, my whole scheme depends on them spotting the "blunder" I made during in the negotiation session.

If no one spots my "mistake," then my plan will collapse around my ears. And quite possibly Butler, Juliet, and I will all be killed.

NAME:
Mulch Diggums

CLASSIFICATION:
Dwarf, Career criminal

BACKGROUND:
Criminal individual who decided early in life that mining was not for him and resolved to put his talents to other uses. Convicted several times for Digging and Entering. Entering the property of Mud People without their permission meant that Mulch forfeited his fairy magic long ago. Like all dwarves, Mulch is terrified of fire.

CRIMINAL RECORD:
Has spent the last three hundred years going in and out of prison

ARRESTING OFFICERS:
Julius Root—eight times. Holly Short—at least once—see "Fei Fei" case file

KNOWN ALIASES:
Lance Digger, the Grouch

KNOWN RELATIONS:
His cousin—Nord

WEAPON OF CHOICE:
His powerful jaws

Mulch Diggums is the only fairy ever to break into the infamous Koboi Laboratories and survive.

CHAPTER 8:
TROLL

FOWL MANOR—CELLAR LEVEL.

JULIET? ARE YOU ALL RIGHT?

QUIET, YOU BIG APE. I'M WATCHING MY FAVORITE WRESTLER, LOUIE THE LOVE MACHINE.

RIGHT. LET'S GO.

NOOO, YOU BIG BULLY. NOT NOW! THIS IS FOR THE INTERCONTINENTAL TITLE.

OH NO.

The humans are going to walk right into the troll...

STAY HERE. IT'S TIME FOR THE PROFESSIONALS TO TAKE OVER.

IF YOU'RE A GOOD BOY, I'LL BUY YOU A LOLLY WHEN I COME BACK.

I tried the doorknob, and got a scorched palm for my trouble.

Sealed.

Captain Short must have blasted it with her weapon.

All I can do is watch.

Butler is expecting a military attack rather than the world's most perfect killing machine.

On any other day, Butler would be halfway up the staircase by now.

On any other day, he wouldn't have Juliet to protect.

The creature is on him in seconds.

Butler gets two shots into the creature's chest; but it just keeps coming.

All I can do is watch.

Lights are offline, so I hit the troll with the only weapon I have left.

My head.

The blow has no effect...

...except for connecting two strands of wire somewhere in the helmet, sending power flooding to one of the lights.

GRRRRRRR

It grabs me and throws me hard.

I feel a rib puncture my lung.

My arm snaps on impact with the floor.

It hurts, but my magic should kick in any second.

Amazingly, the human isn't dead.

A desperate dogged pulse forces blood through his smashed limbs.

Heal.

AND
DON'T COME
BACK.

NAME:
Trolls

CLASSIFICATION:
The most deadly of the deep-tunnel creatures. Trolls wander around the labyrinth of tunnels under the surface of the earth. Any living thing they encounter is likely to end up on the menu.

ENCOUNTERED WHEN:
Occasionally a troll finds its way into the shaft of a pressure elevator. Usually the concentrated air current incinerates them, but in rare instances one survives and is blasted all the way to the surface. Surface exposure to light always drives the troll crazy, sending it on a rampage. The first troll to be captured alive in over a century was caught by Captain Holly Short during its surface rampage in southern Italy.

CRIMSON
PUPILS

RETRACTABLE
CLAWS

BULL TROLL

SNOUT—POWERFUL SENSE OF SMELL,
TUSKS CURVED WITH SERRATED EDGES,
WEAK POINT AT BASE OF SKULL

FULLY GROWN
180 KILOS

I saw it all and I appreciate now, perhaps for the first time, everything that Butler does for me.

CHAPTER 9:
ACE IN THE HOLE

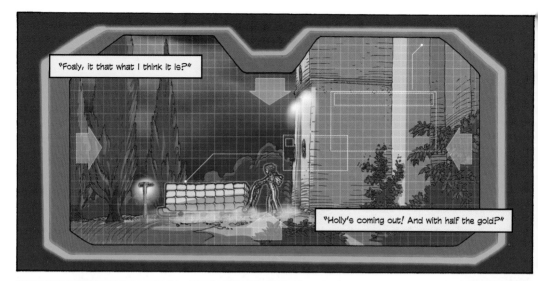

"Foaly, it that what I think it is?"

"Holly's coming out! And with half the gold?"

YOU GAVE IT BACK?

ABOUT HALF. I FELT WE OWED THE CAPTAIN SOMETHING. FOR SERVICES RENDERED.

No need to talk about the wish.

"She's clear."

NOW WE SHOULD CELEBRATE. SOME CHAMPAGNE, I THINK.

"Stand by, Foaly."

I KNOW I'M UNDERAGE, BUT I'M SURE MOTHER WOULDN'T MIND JUST THIS ONCE.

"Launch it."

The tranquilizer hits immediately.

Her embrace is warm and strong.

I feel like a boy again.

I'M SORRY, ARTY. I HAVEN'T BEEN MYSELF FOR THE LAST FEW MONTHS. BUT THINGS ARE GOING TO CHANGE. TIME FOR US TO STOP LIVING IN THE PAST.

My mind is racing. Now that Mother is back, my life is going to change. (We're going to have to explain what happened to the entrance hall, for one thing.)

If my plans are going to escape Mother's attention, then they will have to be even more devious than usual.

I tell Butler that in the future we will restrict ourselves to more tasteful ventures.

I can't promise they'll all be legal, though....

Adapted from the novel *Artemis Fowl*.

Text copyright © 2007 by Eoin Colfer
Illustrations copyright © 2007 by Giovanni Rigano
Fact file art elements by Megan Noller Holt

Printed in the United States of America
First Edition
10 9 8 7 6 5 4 3 2 1
Library of Congress Cataloging-in-Publication Data on file.
ISBN-13: 978-0-7868-4881-2
ISBN-10: 0-7868-4881-2 (hardcover)
ISBN-13: 978-0-7868-4882-9
ISBN-10: 0-7868-4882-0 (paperback)

Visit www.artemisfowl.com and www.hyperionbooksforchildren.com